THE GOLDEN BOOK OF
FUN and NONSENSE

Selected and with commentary by

Louis Untermeyer

illustrated by

Alice and Martin Provensen

A Golden Book • New York

Golden Books Publishing Company, Inc., New York, New York 10106

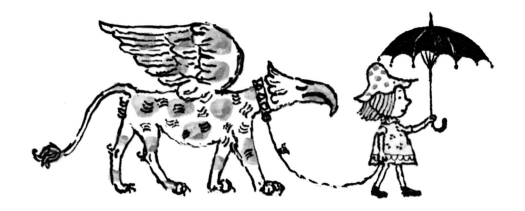

For Karen Anna

ACKNOWLEDGMENTS: The editor and publisher have made every effort to trace the ownership of all copyright material and to obtain permission from the holders of the copyright. Should any question arise as to the use of any selection or any error, the editor and publisher will be glad to make the necessary correction in future printing. Thanks are due to the following publishers, agents, and authors for permission to reprint the material indicated.

ATLANTIC-LITTLE, BROWN AND CO. for "Laughing Time" from *Laughing Time* by William Jay Smith; copyright 1955 by William Jay Smith. Reprinted by permission of the author and publisher.

GERALD DUCKWORTH & CO. LTD. for "Henry King" and "Rebecca" from *Cautionary Tales* by Hilaire Belloc, "The Yak" and "The Elephant" from *The Bad Child's Book of Beasts* by Hilaire Belloc.

ALFRED A. KNOPF, INC. for "Henry King" and "Rebecca" from *Cautionary Tales* by Hilaire Belloc, "The Yak" and "The Elephant" from *The Bad Child's Book of Beasts* by Hilaire Belloc. Published 1941 by Alfred A. Knopf, Inc.

J. B. LIPPINCOTT COMPANY for "Why Nobody Pets the Lion at the Zoo" from *The Reason for the Pelican* by John Ciardi. Copyright 1959 by John Ciardi.

LITTLE, BROWN AND CO. (See Atlantic-Little, Brown and Co.)

DAVID McCORD for "Mr. Bidery's Spidery Garden" by David McCord. Reprinted by permission.

THE SOCIETY OF AUTHORS for "The Bees' Song" from *Peacock Pie* by Walter de la Mare.

The translations and adaptations by Louis Untermeyer are copyright by him.

The poem by Molly Michaels is copyright by Louis Untermeyer.

CONTENTS

A FOREWORD

It is hard to draw the line between comic verse and nonsense poetry, just as it is hard in these commercially crowded, word clashing days to draw the line between sense and nonsense.

We are always ready to chuckle at the exposure of a silly claim or cheer at the toppling of a hollow institution. We laugh at the absurd, the incongruous, the unexpected downfall of what seems pretentious. Some years ago, in an article in the *South Atlantic Quarterly*, Elmer Blistein gave an example of our delight in the reversal of the expected. "At the beginning of a Marx Brothers film, *A Day in Casablanca*, Harpo is discovered leaning against a building. A policeman comes along, asks the inevitable question—'Are you holding this building up?'—but receives the unexpected answer of a smiling, vigorous, affirmative shake of the head. Outraged at the unexpected answer (his routine, you see, has been disrupted), the policeman yanks Harpo away. The building, needless to say, collapses. Our laughter is directed at the policeman, not at Harpo. Not only has the building collapsed, but, if only for a moment, the entire rigid world of officialdom has collapsed."

Nonsense can make no claim to being critical, although frequently it mocks much that is solemn. Sometimes, as in the case of Lewis Carroll's parodies of serious poetry, nonsense unites delightful play and devastating ridicule. The chief aim of nonsense—if anything so lighthearted may have an aim—is a special kind of enjoyment, an enjoyment not to be had from more thoughtful verse. Its true function is fun. Light verse is usually as airy as its name implies, and its test is not the communication of maxims but merriment.

Nevertheless, light verse and nonsense have their own logic. It is not only logical but inevitable that a Pobble with toes should set out to swim the Bristol Channel, lose his toes when the flannel wrapper is snatched from his nose, and then be happier without them in the end. It is logical as well as laughable that a white-haired old man should stand on his head, balance an eel on the end of his nose, and learn law so he can strengthen his jaw by arguing each case with his wife.

These logical absurdities appear in this book supported by many more ludicrous surprises. Here are the wonderful immortal inventions by such classics as Edward Lear and Lewis Carroll. Here also are almost equally hilarious pieces by W. S. Gilbert and Hilaire Belloc, plus a host of less familiar experts in fun and nonsense, like the Carryls, Charles E. and Guy Wetmore. Here, too, are the more modern: Walter de la Mare, who combined a delicate madness with an even more delicate music, along with such contemporaries as David McCord, William Jay Smith, and John Ciardi.

The lightness of light verse charms us because it trips on pretty but precise feet. As for nonsense, only the ignorant will condemn it. The two greatest writers of nonsense were two of the most earnest men of their times. Edward Lear was an authoritative landscape painter, while Lewis Carroll, under his real name of Charles Lutwidge Dodgson, was an ordained deacon who taught mathematics and wrote a series of important books on that abstruse subject. Remember that the great eighteenth-century panjandrum of literature, Samuel Johnson, said, "Any man can write sense. Only the gifted few can write nonsense." Remember, too, that, while "Life is real, life is earnest,"

A little nonsense now and then
Is relished by the best of men.

—Louis Untermeyer

Nonsense goes back a long way. The Greeks had several words for it, and some of the Roman plays are full of a madness that has little method in it. Mother Goose seems to have made a specialty of nonsense rhymes, and the nursery has always sounded their echoes. Nursery rhymes, in fact, have been heard—and enjoyed—by more people than any other form of literature. It has been said that the jingles of our childhood "hum in our ears through life and, in our old age, ring us into eternity."

Here, then, is a sampling of old but not too familiar nonsense nursery rhymes.

SOME LESS FAMILIAR NURSERY RHYMES

Betty, my sister, and I fell out.
    And what do you think it was all about?
She loves coffee and I love tea,
    And that is the reason we couldn't agree.

The Duke of Cumberland,
    He had ten thousand men;
He marched them up to the top of a hill,
    Then marched them down again.

And when they were up, they were up;
    And when they were down, they were down;
And when they were only half-way up,
    They were neither up nor down.

———

Three children skating on the ice
    Upon a summer's day;
As it fell out, they all fell in;
    The rest they ran away.

Now, had those children been at home,
    Or skating on dry ground,
The odds are twenty-five to one
    They had not all been drowned.

You parents all that children have,
    And you, too, that have none,
If you would have them safe abroad,
    Pray keep them safe at home.

———

The man in the wilderness asked of me
    How many strawberries grow in the sea.
I answered him, as I thought good,
    As many as red herrings grow in the wood.

———

Ladybird, ladybird, fly away home!
    Your house is on fire, your children are gone!
All except one, and her name is Anne;
    She crept under the frying pan.

There was an owl lived in an oak.
    The more he heard the less he spoke.
The less he spoke the more he heard.
    Now wasn't that a wise old bird!

———

If all the land were apple pie,
    And all the seas were ink,
And all the trees were bread and cheese,
    What would we have to drink?

NINETEENTH CENTURY NONSENSE

Walter A. Raleigh

I wish I loved the Human Race;
I wish I loved its silly face;
I wish I liked the way it walks;
I wish I liked the way it talks;
And when I'm introduced to one
I wish I thought "What jolly fun!"

James Payne

I never had a piece of toast
    Particularly long and wide,
But fell upon the dirty floor,
    And always on the buttered side.

James Ball Naylor

King David and King Solomon
    Led merry, merry lives,
With many, many lady friends
    And many, many wives.
But when old age crept over them,
    With many, many qualms,
King Solomon wrote the Proverbs,
    And King David wrote the Psalms.

Baron Charles Bowen

The rain it raineth on the just
    And also on the unjust fella.
But chiefly on the just, because
    The unjust steals the just's umbrella.

Samuel Wilberforce

If I were a Cassowary
    On the plains of Timbuctoo,
I would eat a missionary,
    Cassock, band, and hymn-book, too.

Known throughout the world as the author of The Deserted Village *(a pastoral poem),* She Stoops to Conquer *(a play), and* The Vicar of Wakefield *(a novel), Oliver Goldsmith was also a high-hearted humorist, as this poem, packed with word-plays, proves.*

ELEGY ON THE DEATH OF A MAD DOG

Oliver Goldsmith

Good people all, of every sort,
　Give ear unto my song;
And if you find it wondrous short,—
　It cannot hold you long.

In Islington there was a man,
　Of whom the world might say
That still a godly race he ran,—
　Whene'er he went to pray.

A kind and gentle heart he had,
　To comfort friends and foes;
The naked every day he clad,—
　When he put on his clothes.

And in that town a dog was found,
　As many dogs there be,
Both mongrel, puppy, whelp, and hound,
　And curs of low degree.

The dog and man at first were friends;
　But when a pique began,
The dog, to gain some private ends,
　Went mad, and bit the man.

Around from all the neighboring streets,
　The wondering neighbors ran,
And swore the dog had lost his wits
　To bite so good a man.

The wound it seemed both sore and sad
　To every Christian eye;
And while they swore the dog was mad,
　They swore the man would die.

But soon a wonder came to light,
　That showed the rogues they lied;
The man recovered from the bite,
　The dog it was that died.

William Brighty Rands is an almost forgotten nineteenth-century name. Yet, anthologists have ransacked his Lilliput Levee *(published in 1864) for bits of nonsense as amusing as* Topsy-Turvy World.

TOPSY-TURVY WORLD

William Brighty Rands

If the butterfly courted the bee,
  And the owl the porcupine;
If churches were built in the sea,
  And three times one was nine;
If the pony rode his master,
  If the buttercups ate the cows,
If the cat had the dire disaster
  To be worried, sir, by the mouse;
If mama, sir, sold the baby
  To a Gypsy for half a crown;
If a gentleman, sir, was a lady,—
  The world would be Upside-Down!
If any or all of these wonders
  Should ever come about,
I should not consider them blunders,
  For I should be Inside-Out!

THEY TOLD ME YOU HAD BEEN TO HER

Lewis Carroll

Lewis Carroll was a master of logical nonsense; as an expert mathematician he invented the most amazing tricks and curious games. His books were another expression of a fantastically ingenious mind. Through the Looking-Glass *is not only a continually surprising set of puzzles, but it is also a disguised game of chess in which Alice, a white pawn, becomes queen. One of Carroll's favorite tricks was to write poems that made fun of other poems, especially serious poems.* Father William, *for example, is a parody of a moralizing poem by one of England's poet laureates, Robert Southey. Southey's title was (and still is)* The Old Man's Comforts and How He Gained Them. *Everyone has forgotten Southey's old man, but everyone remembers Carroll's.*

A deacon in holy orders and a university lecturer, Lewis Carroll could never get too much of nonsense. Besides the nonsensical logic in Alice's Adventures in Wonderland *and its sequel,* Through the Looking-Glass, *Carroll's skylarking spirit fooled its way through* Sylvie and Bruno, The Hunting of the Snark, *and other phantasmagoria. Carroll wrote at least two versions of the "evidence" read at the trial of the Knave of Hearts in* Alice's Adventures in Wonderland. *The later one is given here.*

They told me you had been to her,
  And mentioned me to him:
She gave me a good character,
  But said I could not swim.

He sent them word I had not gone
  (We know it to be true):
If she should push the matter on,
  What would become of you?

I gave her one, they gave him two,
  You gave us three or more;
They all returned from him to you,
  Though they were mine before.

If I or she should chance to be
  Involved in this affair,
He trusts to you to set them free,
  Exactly as we were.

My notion was that you had been
  (Before she had this fit)
An obstacle that came between
  Him, and ourselves, and it.

Don't let him know she liked them best,
  For this must ever be
A secret, kept from all the rest,
  Between yourself and me.

FATHER WILLIAM

Lewis Carroll

"You are old, Father William," the young man said,
  "And your hair has become very white;
And yet you incessantly stand on your head—
  Do you think at your age it is right?"

"In my youth," Father William replied to his son,
  "I feared it might injure my brain;
But, now that I'm perfectly sure I have none,
  Why, I do it again and again."

"You are old," said the youth, "as I mentioned before,
   And have grown most uncommonly fat;
Yet you turned a back-somersault in at the door—
   Pray, what is the reason for that?"

"In my youth," said the sage, as he shook his grey locks,
   "I kept all my limbs very supple
By the use of this ointment—one shilling the box—
   Allow me to sell you a couple."

"You are old," said the youth, "and your jaws are too weak
   For anything tougher than suet:
Yet you finished the goose, with the bones and the beak—
   Pray, how did you manage to do it?"

"In my youth," said his father, "I took to the law,
   And argued each case with my wife;
And the muscular strength which it gave to my jaw
   Has lasted the rest of my life."

"You are old," said the youth, "one would hardly suppose
   That your eye was as steady as ever;
Yet you balanced an eel on the end of your nose—
   What made you so awfully clever?"

"I have answered three questions, and that is enough,"
   Said his father. "Don't give yourself airs.
Do you think I can listen all day to such stuff?
   Be off, or I'll kick you downstairs!"

JABBERWOCKY

Lewis Carroll

’Twas brillig, and the slithy toves
    Did gyre and gimble in the wabe;
All mimsy were the borogoves,
    And the mome raths outgrabe.

Jabberwocky *should be read—and enjoyed—as pure nonsense. However, for those who require explanation, the author, Lewis Carroll, has offered several tongue-in-cheek definitions. In a chapter of* Through the Looking-Glass, *he has Humpty Dumpty tell Alice that "brillig" means four o'clock in the afternoon, for that is the time when they begin "broiling" and "grilling" things for dinner. The "toves" (which seem to be a mixture of "toads" and "doves") are "slithy" because they are "lithe" and "slimy." To "gyre" is to go round and round like a gyroscope, and to "gimble" is to make holes like a gimlet. The author also explains that "frumious" is a word that happens when you think of "fretful" and "fuming" and "furious" all at the same time—and try to say all three words at once! "Mome" is, of course, short for "from home." As for the other queer words, it might be fun to figure them out for yourself. But, as stated above, the best way to read* Jabberwocky *is to take care of the sounds and let the sense take care of itself.*

"Beware the Jabberwock, my son!
  The jaws that bite, the claws that catch!
Beware the Jubjub bird, and shun
  The frumious Bandersnatch!"

He took his vorpal sword in hand:
  Long time the manxome foe he sought—
So rested he by the Tumtum tree,
  And stood awhile in thought.

And as in uffish thought he stood,
  The Jabberwock, with eyes of flame,
Came whiffling through the tulgey wood,
  And burbled as it came!

One, two! One, two! And through and through
  The vorpal blade went snicker-snack!
He left it dead, and with its head
  He went galumphing back.

"And hast thou slain the Jabberwock?
  Come to my arms, my beamish boy!
O frabjous day! Callooh! Callay!"
  He chortled in his joy.

'Twas brillig, and the slithy toves
  Did gyre and gimble in the wabe;
All mimsy were the borogoves,
  And the mome raths outgrabe.

23

The author of the next poem, Charles E. Carryl, is not to be confused with Lewis Carroll. But Carryl loved the works of Carroll so much that he not only read them to his little boy, Guy (who also turned out to be a brilliant writer—see page 66), but also wrote a sort of new Alice in Wonderland *for him. He called it* Davy and the Goblin. *In it he took old legends and turned them upside down—for instance, Robin Hood is found to be the father of Red Riding Hood, and men from Scotland are Butter-scotchmen. The* Walloping Window-Blind, *sometimes called* A Nautical Ballad, *is one of his liveliest fantasies.*

THE WALLOPING WINDOW-BLIND

Charles E. Carryl

A capital ship for an ocean trip
    Was the "Walloping Window-Blind"—
No gale that blew dismayed her crew
    Or troubled the captain's mind.
The man at the wheel was taught to feel
    Contempt for the wildest blow,
And it often appeared, when the weather had cleared,
    That he'd been in his bunk below.

The boatswain's mate was very sedate,
    Yet fond of amusement, too:
And he played hop-scotch with the starboard watch,
    While the captain tickled the crew.
And the gunner we had was apparently mad,
    For he sat on the after rail,
And fired salutes with the captain's boots,
    In the teeth of the booming gale.

The captain sat in a commodore's hat
   And dined in a royal way
On toasted pigs and pickles and figs
   And gummery bread each day.
But the cook was Dutch and behaved as such:
   For the food that he gave the crew
Was a number of tons of hot-cross buns
   Chopped up with sugar and glue.

And we all felt ill as mariners will,
   On a diet that's cheap and rude;
And we shivered and shook as we dipped the cook
   In a tub of his gluesome food.
Then nautical pride we laid aside,
   And we cast the vessel ashore
On the Gulliby Isles, where the Poohpooh smiles,
   And the Anagazanders roar.

Composed of sand was that favored land,
   And trimmed with cinnamon straws;
And pink and blue was the pleasing hue
   Of the Tickletoeteaser's claws.
And we sat on the edge of a sandy ledge
   And shot at the whistling bee:
And the Binnacle-bats wore waterproof hats
   As they danced in the sounding sea.

On rubagub bark, from dawn to dark,
   We fed, till we all had grown
Uncommonly shrunk,—when a Chinese junk
   Came by from the torriby zone.
She was stubby and square, but we didn't much care,
   As we cheerily put to sea;
And we left the crew of the junk to chew
   The bark of the rubagub tree.

Millions of readers have relished the rollicking rhymes of Edward Lear. But not many of them know that the man who has been hailed as childhood's madcap laureate was a sad and lonely person, a painter whose landscape pictures were so accurate that experts could recognize the geology of the country from his designs, a lithographer whose drawings of birds were compared to Audubon's, and a technician so precise that Queen Victoria engaged him as her drawing-teacher. He achieved extraordinary accomplishments (one of his friends inherited as many as ten thousand drawings) in spite of a lifelong ailment (he was a victim of epilepsy from the age of seven). A sick man and a somber student, Lear was happiest when he was most nonsensical. It is an interesting fact that Lear's grandfather, a Dane, spelled his name Lör, and the equivalent in Greek means "nonsense."

Certain poet-critics maintain that there is much below the surface of Lear's fantasies. T. S. Eliot found a lyric purity in otherwise meaningless lines, and Robert Graves discovered emotional depths in Calico Pie, *whose birds suggest "the familiar emblem of unrealized love." However, no one is urged to take* Calico Pie *or any of the other verses more seriously than Lear intended—and Lear never meant them to be anything more than amusing, musical plays of the imagination.*

CALICO PIE

Edward Lear

Calico Pie
  The little Birds fly
Down to the calico tree,
  Their wings were blue,
  And they sang "Tilly-loo!"
  Till away they flew—
And they never came back to me!
  They never came back!
  They never came back!
They never came back to me!

  Calico Jam
  The little Fish swam
Over the syllabub sea,
  He took off his hat,
  To the Sole and the Sprat,
  And the Willeby-wat—
But he never came back to me!
  He never came back!
  He never came back!
He never came back to me!

  Calico Ban
  The little Mice ran,
To be ready in time for tea,
  Flippity flup,
  They drank it all up,
  And danced in the cup—
But they never came back to me!
  They never came back!
  They never came back!
They never came back to me!

  Calico Drum,
  The Grasshoppers come,
The Butterfly, Beetle, and Bee,
  Over the ground,
  Around and round,
  With a hop and a bound—
But they never came back!
  They never came back!
  They never came back!
They never came back to me!

THE POBBLE WHO HAS NO TOES

Edward Lear

The Pobble who has no toes
   Had once as many as we.
When they said, "Some day you may lose them;"
   He replied, "Fish fiddle de-dee!"
And his Aunt Jobiska made him drink
Lavender water tinged with pink;
For she said, "The world in general knows
There's nothing so good for a Pobble's toes!"

The Pobble who has no toes,
    Swam across the Bristol Channel;
But before he set out he wrapped his nose
    In a piece of scarlet flannel.
For his Aunt Jobiska said, "No harm
Can come to his toes if his nose is warm;
And it's perfectly known that a Pobble's toes
Are safe—provided he minds his nose."

The Pobble swam fast and well,
    And when boats or ships came near him,
He tinkledy-binkledy-winkled a bell
    So that all the world could hear him.
And all the sailors and Admirals cried,
When they saw him nearing the further side—
"He has gone to fish for his Aunt Jobiska's
Runcible Cat with crimson whiskers!"

But before he touched the shore—
  The shore of the Bristol Channel,
A sea-green Porpoise carried away
  His wrapper of scarlet flannel.
And when he came to observe his feet,
Formerly garnished with toes so neat,
His face at once became forlorn
On perceiving that all his toes were gone!

And nobody ever knew,
  From that dark day to the present,
Whoso had taken the Pobble's toes,
  In a manner so far from pleasant.
Whether the shrimps or crawfish grey,
Or crafty Mermaids stole them away,
Nobody knew; and nobody knows
How the Pobble was robbed of his twice five toes!

The Pobble who has no toes
  Was placed in a friendly Bark,
And they rowed him back, and carried him up
  To his Aunt Jobiska's Park.
And she made him a feast, at his earnest wish,
Of eggs and butter cups fried with fish;
And she said, "It's a fact the whole world knows,
That Pobbles are happier without their toes."

THE QUANGLE WANGLE'S HAT

Edward Lear

On the top of the Crumpetty Tree
   The Quangle Wangle sat,
But his face you could not see,
   On account of his Beaver Hat.
For his Hat was a hundred and two feet wide,
With ribbons and bibbons on every side,
And bells, and buttons, and loops, and lace,
So that nobody ever could see the face
   Of the Quangle Wangle Quee.

The Quangle Wangle said
   To himself on the Crumpetty Tree,
"Jam, and jelly, and bread
   Are the best of food for me!
But the longer I live on this Crumpetty Tree
The plainer than ever it seems to me
That very few people come this way
And that life on the whole is far from gay!"
   Said the Quangle Wangle Quee.

But there came to the Crumpetty Tree
   Mr. and Mrs. Canary;
And they said, "Did you ever see
   Any spot so charmingly airy?
May we build a nest on your lovely Hat?
Mr. Quangle Wangle, grant us that!
Oh, please let us come and build a nest,
Of whatever material suits you best,
   Mr. Quangle Wangle Quee!"

And besides, to the Crumpetty Tree
   Came the Stork, the Duck, and the Owl;
The Snail and the Bumble Bee,
   The Frog and the Fimble Fowl
(The Fimble Fowl, with a corkscrew leg);
And all of them said, "We humbly beg
We may build our homes on your lovely Hat—
Mr. Quangle Wangle, grant us that!
   Mr. Quangle Wangle Quee!"

And the Golden Grouse came there,
  And the Pobble who has no toes,
And the small Olympian Bear,
  And the Dong with a luminous nose.
And the Blue Baboon who played the flute,
And the Orient Calf from the Land of Tute,
And the Attery Squash, and the Bisky Bat—
All came and built on the lovely Hat
  Of the Quangle Wangle Quee!

And the Quangle Wangle said
  To himself on the Crumpetty Tree,
"When all these creatures move
  What a wonderful noise there'll be!"
And at night by the light of the Mulberry Moon
They danced to the Flute of the Blue Baboon,
On the broad green leaves of the Crumpetty Tree,
And all were as happy as happy could be,
  With the Quangle Wangle Quee.

Although many believe that Edward Lear invented the limerick, limericks appeared long before his time. Several old nursery rhymes consisted of the odd five-line form which became famous. Here is one of them:

As a little fat man of Bombay
Was smoking one very hot day,
A bird called a snipe
Flew away with his pipe,
Which vexed that fat man of Bombay.

If Lear did not invent the limerick, he popularized it. To entertain children (and himself) he wrote more than two hundred ridiculous rhymes full of laughable situations. Three examples by "Queery Leary" follow.

THREE LIMERICKS

Edward Lear

There was an old man of Peru,
Who watched his wife making a stew.
   But once by mistake
   In a stove she did bake,
That unfortunate man of Peru.

There was an old man who said, "Hush!
I perceive a young bird in this bush!"
   When they said "Is it small?"
   He replied, "Not at all!
It is four times as big as this bush!"

There was an old man in a tree
Who was horribly bored by a bee.
   When they said "Does it buzz?"
   He replied, "Yes it does!
It's a regular brute of a bee!"

After Lear showed how easy it was to make up limericks, everyone wrote them. People not only imitated Lear's verses but also improved on them. Lear's limericks always ended with the same word that ended either the first or second line; after Lear, the last line had a new rhyme. It gave the limerick a surprising turn and added a more humorous twist. Here are six favorites.

SIX LIMERICKS AFTER LEAR

A diner while dining at Crewe
Found a rather large mouse in his stew.
   Said the waiter, "Don't shout
   And wave it about,
Or the rest will be wanting one, too."

A handsome young noble of Spain
Met a lion one day in the rain.
   He ran in a fright
   With all of his might,
But the lion, he ran with his mane!

There was a young girl, a sweet lamb,
Who smiled as she entered a tram.
    After she had embarked
    The conductor remarked,
"Your fare!" And she said, "Yes, I am."

There was an old man of Blackheath
Who sat on his set of false teeth.
    Said he, with a start,
    "O, Lord, bless my heart!
I have bitten myself underneath!"

There was a young fellow named Green,
Whose musical sense was not keen.
    He said, "It is odd,
    But I cannot tell *God
Save the Weasel* from *Pop Goes the Queen!*"

There was an old man of Peru,
Who dreamt he was eating his shoe.
    He awoke in the night
    In a horrible fright,
And found it was perfectly true!

Then there are the tongue-twisting limericks. Carolyn Wells was expert in this tricky form.

TWO TONGUE TWISTERS

Carolyn Wells

A canner exceedingly canny
One morning remarked to his granny,
  "A canner can can
  Anything that he can,
But a canner can't can a can, can he?"

A tutor who tooted the flute
Tried to tutor two tooters to toot.
  Said the two to the tutor,
  "Is it harder to toot, or
To tutor two tooters to toot?"

Some of the funniest (and also most horrifying) little verses were written by a person who signed himself Col. D. Streamer. His real name was Harry Graham; he took his pen name from a regiment to which he belonged: the Coldstream Guards. His Ruthless Rhymes for Heartless Homes *were quoted with fiendish delight, copied, and imitated throughout the English-speaking world. Graham's most popular quatrain was about a boy called Billy, and the imitations became known as "Little Willies."*

RANDOM RUTHLESS RHYMES

The first four ruthless rhymes are by Graham himself; the other three are by unknown contributors to the savage saga.

Billy, in one of his nice, new sashes,
Fell in the fire and was burnt to ashes.
Now, although the room grows chilly,
I haven't the heart to poke at Billy.

———

"There's been an accident," they said.
"Your servant's cut in half. He's dead!"
"Indeed!" said Mr. Jones. "And please
Send me the half that's got my keys."

———

Father heard his children scream,
So he threw them in the stream,
Saying, as he drowned the third,
"Children should be seen, not heard!"

———

In the drinking well
Which the plumber built her,
Aunt Eliza fell.
    We must buy a filter.

Willie poisoned his father's tea;
Father died in agony.
Mother came, and looked quite vexed:
"Really, Will," she said, "what next?"

———

Willie saw some dynamite,
Couldn't understand it quite;
Curiosity never pays.
It rained Willie seven days.

———

Making toast at the fireside
Nurse fell in the grate and died.
But what makes it ten times worse,
All the toast was burnt with Nurse.

40

The Clerihew is a comparatively new form of verse. It got its name from its inventor, a writer of detective stories, E. C. Bentley, whose middle name was Clerihew. Clerihews are short; they are never more than four lines and they always begin with the name of a famous character. But the facts about him are seldom right. In fact, they are grotesquely—and purposely—wrong. The first three are by Bentley himself; the other three are by Louis Untermeyer.

THREE CLERIHEWS

Edward the Confessor
Slept under the dresser.
When that began to pall,
He slept in the hall.

———

Said Sir Christopher Wren,
"I'm having lunch with some men.
If anyone calls,
Say I'm designing Saint Paul's."

———

When Alexander Pope
Accidentally trod on the soap,
And came down on the back of his head—
Never mind what he said.

THREE MORE CLERIHEWS

Alfred, Lord Tennyson
Lived upon venison;
Not cheap, I fear,
Because venison's deer.

Francesca de Rimini
Lived in a chiminey,
Full of ghouls in the gloam.
But still, home is home.

Although the Borgias
Were rather gorgeous,
They liked the absurder
Kind of murder.

RULES AND REGULATIONS

From *Useful and Instructive Poetry*

Lewis Carroll

A short direction
To avoid dejection,
By variations
In occupations,

And prolongation
Of relaxation,

And combinations
Of recreations,

And disputation
On the state of the nation

In adaptation
To your station,

By invitations
To friends and relations,

By evitation
Of amputation,

By permutation
In conversation,

And deep reflection
You'll avoid dejection.

Learn well your grammar,
And never stammer,

Write well and neatly, And sing most sweetly, Be enterprising, Love early rising,

Go walk of six miles,
Have ready quick smiles,
With lightsome laughter,
Soft flowing after.

Drink tea, not coffee;
Never eat toffy.
Eat bread with butter.
Once more, don't stutter.

Don't waste your money,
Abstain from honey,
Shut doors behind you,
(Don't slam them, mind you.)

Drink beer, not porter.
Don't enter the water
Till to swim you are able.
Sit close to the table.
Take care of a candle.
Shut a door by the handle,
Don't push with your shoulder
Until you are older.

Lose not a button.
Refuse cold mutton.
Starve your canaries.
Believe in fairies.

If you are able,
Don't have a stable
With any mangers.
Be rude to strangers.

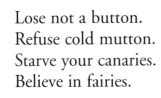

Moral:

BEHAVE!

Heinrich Hoffman, the author of Der Struwwelpeter *(usually translated as* Shock-Headed Peter*), was not a professional author. He was a nineteenth-century German doctor who, unable to find the kind of teaching book he wanted for his young son, decided to make one himself. It was a highly instructive (and rather gruesome) affair. It told about little boys who sucked thumbs and were punished by having their thumbs cut off; about children who made fun of other children who happened to be black and, as a penalty, were plunged into a barrel of ink and emerged blacker than crows; about a boy who went around with his nose stuck in the air, fell in the water and was almost drowned; and other "moral" fables about careless children. No one was more surprised than the doctor himself when* Der Struwwelpeter *went into edition after edition and was reprinted throughout Europe to impress (or frighten) children with what Hoffman called "funny stories."*

The stories which follow emphasize the fun, rather than the cruelty, of the warning tales. Adapted by the editor, they are followed by a few of Hilaire Belloc's "cautionary tales," which carry the lessons of Struwwelpeter *to complete absurdity.*

THE STORY OF CASPAR AND THE SOUP

Heinrich Hoffman

Adapted by Louis Untermeyer

Caspar was never sick at all;
His body was a butter-ball;
Solid he was from head to feet;
His cheeks were red. He loved to eat.
Yet suddenly one dismal day
His parents heard young Caspar say:
"I don't want soup. Take it away!
No soup!" he screamed. "Take it away!
No matter what! No matter when!
I'll never drink a drop again!"

Next day he would not touch his dinner
And—as you see—he grew much thinner.
But still he cried, "I beg and pray,
Remove the stuff! Take it away!
I will not eat my soup today!"

Then, on the third day of the week
Caspar began to pale and peak.
But, as the soup came to the table,
He screamed as loud as he was able:
"Remove the plate! Take it away!
I will not eat my soup today!
I will *not* eat my soup today!"

When four more soupless days had passed
Caspar was skin and bones at last.
He was not thicker than a thread.
And on the fifth day he was dead.
Burying the boy they could not save,
They put a soup-plate on his grave.

THE STORY OF PAULINE AND THE MATCHES

Heinrich Hoffman

Adapted by Louis Untermeyer

Pauline was all alone one day—
Both of her parents were away—
And, having little else to do,
She went from room to room. The view
Was nothing much until she spied
Some matches by the fireside.
"Aha!" she cried. "This will be fun!
And when they all burst into light
They'll blaze and make a lovely sight!"

But Minz and Maunz, those clever cats,
Lifted their paws and told her, "That's
Not like a toy. 'Twill scratch and spit—
Your father has forbidden it.
Pauline, put down those matches now,
Or you'll be hurt. Miaow! Miaow!"

But Pauline would not listen. She
Struck the first match and jumped with glee.
It snapped and crackled loud and clear.
It burned—just like the picture here—
And, as the spark burst into bloom,
Gay Pauline danced around the room.

But Minz and Maunz, those clever cats,
Lifted their paws and told her, "That's
A foolish way for you to act.
You'll get in trouble. That's a fact.
There's one thing everyone has learned:
You play with fire, and you'll get burned.
Put out the flame and do it now.
Miaow! Miaow! Miaow! Miaow!"

Pauline stood still. Too late! The fire
Caught at her clothes and then climbed higher,
It found her hands; it reached her hair.

It burned poor Pauline everywhere.
Then little Minz and Maunz grew wild
And screamed, "Will no one save this child?
Before she draws another breath,
Won't someone save Pauline from death?
Someone must come at once, somehow!
Miaow! Miaow! Miaow! Miaow!"

But no one came. And poor Pauline
Was now consumed. All that was seen
Of what were stockings, strings, and sashes,
Was a pair of shoes and a pile of ashes.

Minz and Maunz, those sorrowful cats,
Mourned at the heap and whimpered, "That's
The bitter lesson for today.
Whatever will her parents say?
Meanwhile, we weep for her." Their tears
Made a small pool. It stayed for years.

THE STORY OF FIDGETY PHILIP

Heinrich Hoffman   *Adapted by* Louis Untermeyer

One evening Philip's father said,
"You twist and squirm and shake your head.
Come, let us see if you are able
To sit quite still for once at table."
But not a word
Had Philip heard.
He giggled
And wiggled
And wriggled
And tottered
And teetered
And rocked in his chair.
Till his father cried, "Philip!

Sit still—or beware!"
Caring nothing for disaster,
Backwards, forwards, always faster,
Philip rocked—until the chair
Slipped from under. Then and there
Philip grabbed the tablecloth,
Spilling everything: the broth,
Bread and butter, all the dishes,
Goblets, gravy, meat and fishes,
Cauliflower, garden greens,
Spinach, parsnips, peas and beans,
Pastry, puddings white and brown . . .
Everything came tumbling down!

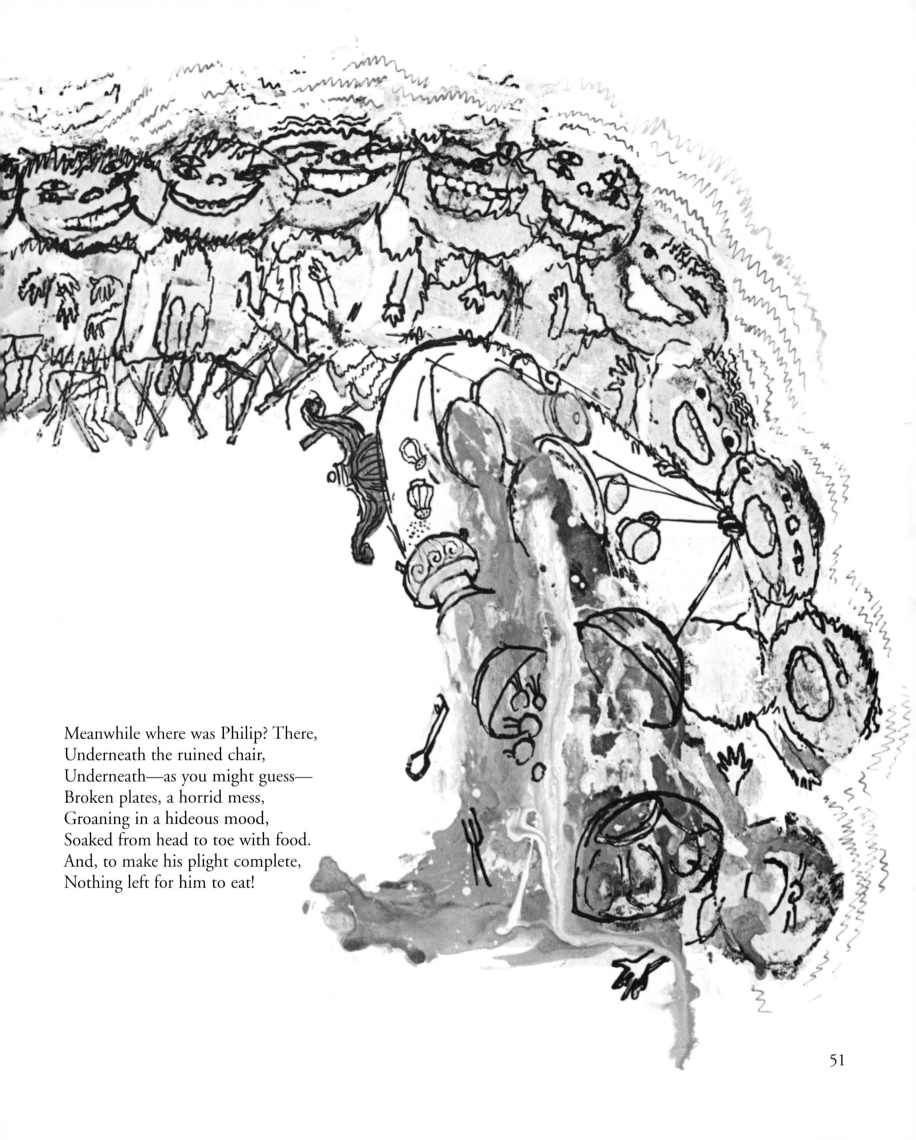

Meanwhile where was Philip? There,
Underneath the ruined chair,
Underneath—as you might guess—
Broken plates, a horrid mess,
Groaning in a hideous mood,
Soaked from head to toe with food.
And, to make his plight complete,
Nothing left for him to eat!

51

Hilaire Belloc, one of the most versatile writers of the late nineteenth century, was a historian, an essayist, a novelist, a politician, a poet, and the author of some of the most delightfully absurd books ever written. The Bad Child's Book of Beasts and More Beasts for Worse Children are superbly nonsensical, and Cautionary Tales continues to be as much relished by grown-ups as by youngsters. There is an ageless humor in the Tales, which are primerlike fables turned upside down—takeoffs on strictly moral verses and "improving" poems, such as those on pages 47-51. With unconcealed glee they relate what happens to children who chew little bits of string, who slam doors, who play with dangerous toys, and who do not do as they are told. More Belloc appears on pages 73 and 75.

HENRY KING

Hilaire Belloc

The Chief Defect of Henry King
Was chewing little bits of String.
At last he swallowed some which tied
Itself in ugly Knots inside.

Physicians of the Utmost Fame
Were called at once; but when they came
They answered, as they took their Fees,
"There is no Cure for this Disease.

Henry will very soon be dead."
His Parents stood about his Bed
Lamenting his Untimely Death,
When Henry, with his Latest Breath,

Cried, "Oh, my Friends, be warned by me,
That Breakfast, Dinner, Lunch, and Tea
Are all the Human Frame requires. . . ."
With that, the Wretched Child expires.

REBECCA

Hilaire Belloc

A Trick that everyone abhors
In Little Girls is Slamming Doors.
A Wealthy Banker's Little Daughter
Who lived in Palace Green, Bayswater
(By name Rebecca Offendort),
Was given to this Furious Sport.
She would deliberately go
And Slam the Door like Billy-Ho!
To make her Uncle Jacob start.
She really was not bad at heart,
But only rather rude and wild.
She was an Aggravating Child.

It happened that a Marble Bust
Of Abraham was standing just
Above the Door this little Lamb
Had carefully prepared to Slam.
And down it came! It knocked her flat!
It laid her out! She looked like that!

Her Funeral Sermon (which was long
And followed by a Sacred Song)
Mentioned her Virtues, it is true,
But dwelt upon her Vices, too,
And showed the Dreadful End of One
Who goes and Slams the Door for Fun.

I soared to my feet; it was still dim.
The moon, like an opal in fright,
Leaned over and whispered, "I killed him
Last night."

Not an hour to lose; I would save her.
I fastened my spurs in the air
With the scent of the twilight I gave her
To wear.

I turned to the parlor in panic
And blurted out, "What must you think?"
She rippled, "Then let me the canak-
in clink!"

Louis Untermeyer is the author, compiler or editor of a hundred books of prose and poetry, including this one.

SURREAL ADVENTURE

Louis Untermeyer

As I thought, with a shriek, of how Friday
  Would burst into corduroy pants.
And I drove like a fiend as I cried, "Day,
         Advance!"

The wind smacked its lips, "Here's a nice treat!"
  The sea was a forest of flame . . .
And so to the billowy Bye Street
         I came.

The stars at my shoulder were baying;
  I surged through a hole in the gate;
And I knew that the Bishop was saying,
         "Too late."

They tell me that no one believed me;
  I never was asked to the feast.
My dears, 'twas the butler deceived me—
         The beast!

Gelett Burgess and Henry S. Leigh specialized in odd ideas and put them into odd verses. Both wrote absurd things with straightforward faces. Gelett Burgess' Purple Cow was not only, as he says, a "mythic beast" but also the subject of one of the most quoted poems of all time.

THE PURPLE COW *'s Projected Feast:*

Reflections on a Mythic Beast,
Who's Quite Remarkable at Least.

I never saw a Purple Cow,
   I never hope to see one:
But I can tell you, anyhow,
   I'd rather see than be one.

THE FLOORLESS ROOM: *A Novel Sort*
Of Argument Without Support.

I Wish that my Room had a Floor!
I don't so Much Care for a Door,
   But this Crawling Around
   Without Touching the Ground
Is getting to be Quite a Bore!

THE WINDOW PAIN: *A Theme Symbolic,*
Pertaining to the Melon Colic.

The Window has Four Little Panes;
   But One have I—
The Window Pains are in its Sash;
   I Wonder Why!

Gelett Burgess

ON DIGITAL EXTREMITIES:
A Poem, and a Gem It Is!

I'd Rather have Fingers than Toes;
I'd Rather Have Ears than a Nose;
  And As for my Hair,
  I'm Glad it's All There;
I'll be Awfully Sad when it goes!

THE SUNSET:
Picturing the Glow It Casts Upon a Dish of Dough.

The Sun is Low, to Say the Least,
  Although it is Well-Red;
Yet, Since it Rises in the Yeast,
  It Should be Better Bred.

THE TWINS

Henry S. Leigh

In form and feature, face and limb,
  I grew so like my brother,
That folks got taking me for him
  And each for one another.
It puzzled all our kith and kin,
  It reached an awful pitch;
For one of us was born a twin,
  Yet not a soul knew which.

One day (to make the matter worse),
  Before our names were fixed,
As we were being washed by nurse
  We got completely mixed;
And thus, you see, by Fate's decree,
  (Or rather nurse's whim),
My brother John got christened *me,*
  And I got christened *him.*

This fatal likeness even dogged
  My footsteps when at school,
And I was always getting flogged,
  For John turned out a fool.
I put this question hopelessly
  To every one I knew—
What *would* you do, if you were me,
  To prove that you were *you?*

Our close resemblance turned the tide
  Of my domestic life;
For somehow my intended bride
  Became my brother's wife.
In short, year after year the same
  Absurd mistakes went on;
And when I died—the neighbors came
  And buried brother John!

CLARA CODD
AND
FREDERICK FRIDDLE

Molly Michaels

Has anyone heard the remarkable riddle
Of Clara Codd and Frederick Friddle?
They started for March, but all unwary
Got lost in the twenty-ninth of February.

Then Clara Codd cried to Frederick Friddle,
"We can go no further; we are stuck in the middle.
My head is spinning, and I don't dare nod."
"Why nod?" said Frederick to Clara Codd.

"Frederick Friddle, Frederick Friddle,
What have you done with your fifty-cent fiddle?"
"I traded the bow for a fishing rod
To catch you a shooting-star, Clara Codd."

"But I can't get a nibble," said Frederick Friddle,
"While the moon is a crust on the night's cold griddle.
We are two lost peas in a heavenly pod."
"Well, what could be nicer?" said Clara Codd.

And there he floats, poor Frederick Friddle,
(Who everyone said was a queer individ'l),

And only astronomers can see that odd
Careless and curious Clara Codd.

*Molly Michaels is a pseudonym which a well-known
writer uses for his lighter moments.*

THE TWELVE-ELF

Christian Morgenstern

Adapted by Louis Untermeyer

The Twelve-elf raises his left hand,
And midnight strikes throughout the land.

Big-mouthed and anxious lies the Bog;
The Chasm moans like a beaten Dog;

The hard Snail crouches in his house;
Fear overcomes the Mealymouse;

Dishes rattle on every shelf;
The Will-o'-the wisp's afraid of himself,

Sophie, the servant, turns in her sleep;
The Planets huddle like lost sheep;

Two Moles dig north instead of south;
Rising Rivers complain of drouth;

The Pot of Broth goes up in steam;
A Nightmare has a horrid dream;

"Prepare," a Raven screams, "your claws
Becaws . . . becaws . . . becaws . . . becaws . . ."

The Twelve-elf yawns, and drops his hand—
And Quiet comforts the sleeping land.

Christian Morgenstern was a German philosopher-poet who experienced a profound spiritual development and wrote a great deal of superior nonsense. His whimsical way with words has been compared to what Paul Klee did with paint. He enjoyed liberating the mind from the world of matter so that inanimate and grotesque things could take on curious but somehow human characteristics.

Hughes Mearns was a scholar, a poet, and a much-admired educator. Yet nothing he ever wrote was quoted, reprinted, and anthologized as much as the four lines that follow—often credited to "Anonymous."

THE LITTLE MAN

Hughes Mearns

As I was walking up the stair
I met a man who wasn't there.
He wasn't there again today.
I wish, I wish, he'd stay away.

A NIGHTMARE

From *Iolanthe*

W. S. Gilbert

One half of the team of Gilbert and Sullivan, W. S. Gilbert not only furnished the plots and lyrics of such comic operas as H.M.S. Pinafore, The Pirates of Penzance, *and* The Mikado, *but also heightened the comedy with rollicking rhymes. Some of his most absurd effects are found in* A Nightmare.

When you're lying awake with a dismal headache, and
    repose is taboo'd by anxiety,
I conceive you may use any language you choose to indulge
    in, without impropriety;
For your brain is on fire—the bedclothes conspire of usual
    slumber to plunder you;
First your counterpane goes and uncovers your toes, and
    your sheet slips demurely from under you;
Then the blanketing tickles—you feel like mixed pickles, so
    terribly sharp is the pricking,
And you're hot, and you're cross, and you tumble and toss
    till there's nothing 'twixt you and the ticking.
Then the bedclothes all creep to the ground in a heap, and
    you pick 'em all up in a tangle;
Next your pillow resigns and politely declines to remain at its
    usual angle!
Well, you get some repose in the form of a doze, with hot
    eye-balls and head ever aching,
But your slumbering teems with such horrible dreams that
    you'd very much better be waking.
For you dream you are crossing the Channel, and tossing
    about in a steamer from Harwich,*
Which is something between a large bathing machine and a
    very small second-class carriage,
And you're giving a treat (penny ice and cold meat) to a
    party of friends and relations—
They're a ravenous horde—and they all came on board at
    Sloane Square and South Kensington Stations.
And bound on that journey you find your attorney (who
    started that morning from Devon);
He's a bit undersized, and you don't feel surprised when he
    tells you he's only eleven.
Well, you're driving like mad with this singular lad (by-the-
    bye, the ship's now a four-wheeler),
And you're playing round games, and he calls you bad names
    when you tell him that "ties pay the dealer";
But this you can't stand, so you throw up your hand, and
    you find you're as cold as an icicle,
In your shirt and your socks (the black silk with gold clocks),
    crossing Salisbury Plain on a bicycle:

*Harwich is pronounced, as you can see from the next line, to rhyme with "carriage."

And he and the crew are on bicycles too—which they've
    somehow or other invested in—
And he's telling the tars all the particu*lars* of a company he's
    interested in—
It's a scheme of devices, to get at low prices, all goods from
    cough mixtures to cables
(Which tickled the sailors) by treating retailers, as though they
    were all vege*tables*—
You get a good spadesman to plant a small tradesman (first
    take off his boots with a boot-tree),
And his legs will take root, and his fingers will shoot, and
    they'll blossom and bud like a fruit tree—
From the greengrocer tree you get grapes and green pea,
    cauliflower, pineapple and cranberries,
While the pastry-cook plant, cherry brandy will grant, apple
    puffs, and three-corners, and banberries—
The shares are a penny, and ever so many are taken by
    Rothschild and Baring,
And just as a few are allotted to you, you awake with a
    shudder despairing—
You're a regular wreck, with a crick in your neck, and no
    wonder you snore, for your head's on the floor, and you've
    needles and pins from your soles to your shins, and your
    flesh is a-creep, for your left leg's asleep, and you've a cramp
    in your toes, and a fly on your nose, and some fluff in your
    lung, and a feverish tongue, and a thirst that's intense, and a
    general sense that you haven't been sleeping in clover;
But the darkness has passed, and it's daylight at last, and the
    night has been long—ditto, ditto my song—and thank
    goodness they're both of them over!

Continually playing with words—and the frequent contradiction between their sound and their sense—David McCord invented drolleries in the lightest verse. Some of his nimblest effects can be found in Take Sky, Odds Without Ends *and* What's More.

MR. BIDERY'S SPIDERY GARDEN

David McCord

Poor old Mr. Bidery.
His garden's awfully spidery:
Bugs use it as a hidery.

In April it was seedery,
By May a mess of weedery;
And oh, the bugs! How greedery!

White flowers out or buddery,
Potatoes made it spuddery;
And when it rained, what muddery!

June days grow long and shaddery;
Bullfrog forgets his taddery;
The spider legs his laddery.

With cabbages so odory,
Snapdragon soon explodery,
At twilight all is toadary.

Young corn still far from foddery,
No sign of goldenroddary,
Yet feeling low and doddery

Is poor old Mr. Bidery,
His garden lush and spidery,
His apples green, not cidery.

Pea-picking *is* so poddery!

Guy Wetmore Carryl, son of Charles E. Carryl (see page 24), surpassed his father when it came to light verse. In Fables for the Frivolous *he played around with the fables of Aesop and La Fontaine. In* Mother Goose for Grown-Ups *he made the old nursery rhymes jump through hoops. He not only added strange twists and queer rhymes, but also supplied odd morals that ended in puns. As a matter of fact, all his fancies were full of puns.*

THE EMBARRASSING EPISODE OF LITTLE MISS MUFFET

Guy Wetmore Carryl

Little Miss Muffet discovered a tuffet,
  (Which never occurred to the rest of us)
And, as 'twas a June day, and just about noonday,
  She wanted to eat—like the best of us;
Her diet was whey, and I hasten to say
  It is wholesome and people grow fat on it.
The spot being lonely, the lady not only
  Discovered the tuffet, but sat on it.

A rivulet gabbled beside her and babbled,
  As rivulets always are thought to do,
And dragonflies sported around and cavorted,
  As poets say dragonflies ought to do;
When, glancing aside for a moment, she spied
  A horrible sight that brought fear to her,
A hideous spider was sitting beside her,
  And most unavoidably near to her!

Albeit unsightly, this creature politely
  Said: "Madam, I earnestly vow to you,
I'm penitent that I did not bring my hat. I
  Should otherwise certainly bow to you."
Though anxious to please, he was so ill at ease
  That he lost all his sense of propriety,
And grew so inept that he clumsily stept
  In her plate—which is barred in Society.

This curious error completed her terror;
  She shuddered, and growing much paler, not
Only left her tuffet, but dealt him a buffet
  Which doubled him up in a sailor knot.
It should be explained that at this he was pained:
  He cried: "I have vexed you, no doubt of it!
Your fist's like a truncheon." "You're still in my luncheon,"
  Was all that she answered. "Get out of it!"

And the MORAL is this: Be it madam or miss
  To whom you have something to say,
You are only absurd when you get in the curd,
  But you're rude when you get in the whey!

Few poets of our time—or any other time—have made lovelier music than Walter de la Mare. He was a time-traveler; he explored the unknown territory beyond the world's end. Perceiving things with a child's vision, he revealed the commonplace with a sense of wonder, turning sense into nonsense and back again.

THE BEES' SONG

Walter de la Mare

Thouzandz of thornz there be
On the Rozez where gozez
The Zebra of Zee:
Sleek, striped, and hairy,
The steed of the Fairy
Princess of Zee.

Heavy with blozzomz be
The Rozez that growzez
In the thickets of Zee,
Where grazez the Zebra,
Marked Abracadeeebra
Of the Princess of Zee.

And he nozez the poziez
Of the Rozez that growzez
So luvez'm and free,
With an eye, dark and wary,
In search of a Fairy,
Whose Rozez he knowzez
Were not honeyed for he,
But to breathe a sweet incense
To solace the Princess
Of far-away Zee.

THE BIRDS' COURTING

Old American Folk Song

"Hi!" said the blackbird, swinging on the air,
"Once I courted a lady fair;
She proved fickle and turned her back,
And ever since then I've dressed in black."

"Hi!" said the furry, leather-winged bat,
"I will tell you the reason that,
The reason that I fly in the night
Is because I lost my heart's delight."

"Hi!" said the little mourning-dove,
"I'll tell you how to regain her love:
Court her night and court her day,
Never give her time to turn away."

"Hi!" said the wood-pecker, drilling on a bench,
"Once I courted a handsome wench;
She got flighty and from me fled,
And ever since then my head's been red."

"Hi!" said the blue-jay, bluer than blue,
"If I was a young man I'd have *two!*
If one proved faithless and chanced for to go,
I'd have another string to my bow."

HOW TO TELL THE WILD ANIMALS

Carolyn Wells

If ever you should go by chance
  To jungles in the East;
And if there should to you advance
  A large and tawny beast,
If he roars at you as you're dyin'
  You'll know it is the Asian Lion.

Or if some time when roaming round,
  A noble wild beast greets you,
With black stripes on a yellow ground,
  Just notice if he eats you.
This simple rule may help you learn
  The Bengal Tiger to discern.

If strolling forth, a beast you view,
  Whose hide with spots is peppered,
As soon as he has leapt on you,
  You'll know it is the Leopard.
'Twill do no good to roar with pain,
  He'll only lep and lep again.

If when you're walking round your yard,
  You meet a creature there,
Who hugs you very, very hard,
  Be sure it is the Bear.
If you have any doubt, I guess
  He'll give you just one more caress.

Though to distinguish beasts of prey
　　A novice might nonplus,
The Crocodiles you always may
　　Tell from Hyenas thus:
Hyenas come with merry smiles;
　　But if they weep, they're Crocodiles.

The true Chameleon is small,
　　A lizard sort of thing;
He hasn't any ears at all,
　　And not a single wing.
If there is nothing in the tree,
　　'Tis the Chameleon you see.

THE ELEPHANT

Hilaire Belloc

When people call this beast to mind,
  They marvel more and more
At such a little tail behind.
  So LARGE a trunk before.

Poet, essayist, lecturer, translator, and editor, John Ciardi endeared himself to children with the nonsense verses of The Reason for the Pelican *and* The Man Who Sang the Sillies. *The following absurdity is from the latter volume.*

WHY NOBODY PETS THE LION AT THE ZOO

John Ciardi

The morning that the world began
The Lion growled a growl at Man.

And I suspect the Lion might
(If he'd been closer) have tried a bite.

I think that's as it ought to be
And not as it was taught to me.

I think the Lion has a right
To growl a growl and bite a bite.

And if the Lion bothered Adam,
He should have growled right back at 'im.

The way to treat a Lion right
Is growl for growl and bite for bite.

True, the Lion is better fit
For biting than for being bit.

But if you look him in the eye
You'll find the Lion's rather shy.

He really wants someone to pet him.
The trouble is: his teeth won't let him.

He has a heart of gold beneath
But the Lion just can't trust his teeth.

THE YAK

Hilaire Belloc

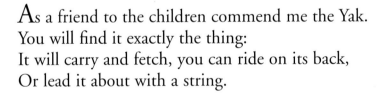

As a friend to the children commend me the Yak.
You will find it exactly the thing:
It will carry and fetch, you can ride on its back,
Or lead it about with a string.

The Tartar who dwells on the plains of Thibet
(A desolate region of snow)
Has for centuries made it a nursery pet,
And surely the Tartar should know!

Then tell your papa where the Yak can be got,
And if he is awfully rich,
He will buy you the creature—or else he will not.
(I cannot be positive which.)

William Jay Smith is a many-sided creator. He is not only a poet, critic, teacher, and translator, but also the author of half a dozen popular books for the very young. Laughing Time *is the title poem of one of them.*

LAUGHING TIME

William Jay Smith

It was laughing time, and the tall Giraffe
Lifted his head, and began to laugh:

Ha! Ha! Ha! Ha!

And the Chimpanzee on the gingko tree
Swung merrily down with a Tee Hee Hee:

Hee! Hee! Hee! Hee!

"It's certainly not against the law!"
Croaked Justice Crow with a loud guffaw:

Haw! Haw! Haw! Haw!

The dancing Bear who could never say "No"
Waltzed up and down on the tip of his toe:

Ho! Ho! Ho! Ho!

The Donkey daintily took his paw,
And around they went: Hee-Haw! Hee-Haw!

Hee-Haw! Hee-Haw!

The Moon had to smile as it started to climb;
All over the world it was laughing time!

Ho! Ho! Ho! Ho! Hee-Haw! Hee-Haw!
Hee! Hee! Hee! Hee! Ha! Ha! Ha! Ha!